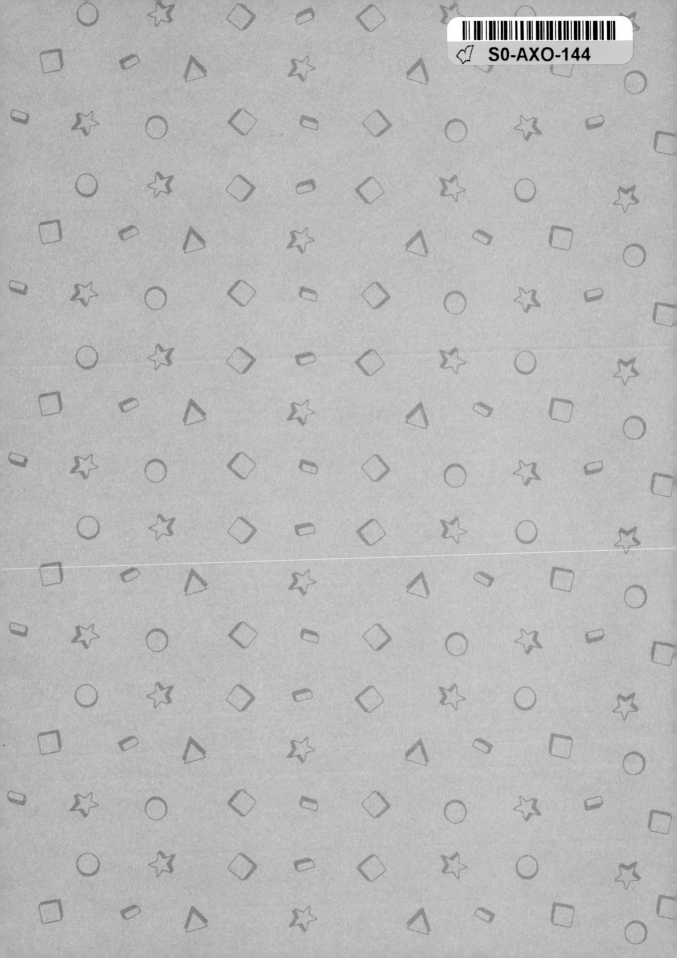

HUEY, DEWEY, AND LOUIE IN SPACE

A Book About Shapes

By Michael Teitelbaum
Illustrated by Darrell Baker

A GOLDEN BOOK • NEW YORK
Western Publishing Company, Inc., Racine, Wisconsin 53404

A B C D E F G H I J K L M

Huey, Dewey, and Louie were strapped into the cockpit of their rocket ship, ready for takeoff.

"Everything's set!" said Huey.

"All systems are go!" said Dewey.

"3-2-1—blast off!" counted Louie. With a loud roar, the ship took off into the night sky.

"What's our mission, fellas?" asked Louie.

"We're traveling to the Planet of the Shapes!" said Huey. "The shape people, who live there, are in trouble."

"Yeah," added Dewey. "A nasty old creature that likes to eat shapes has been gobbling up the shape people. We've got to stop it!"

"According to the planetary map in *The Junior
Woodchuck Guidebook,*" began Huey, "we should set our
course like this." Huey pressed a button on the control
panel.

Suddenly the ship went spinning off course.

"Hey!" shouted Dewey. "You must have pressed the
wrong button!"

"Quick," said Louie. "Turn the dial that's in the shape of a **circle**!"

Huey turned the **circle** dial, but the ship started heading straight down.

"Wrong again!" said Dewey. "Try the **square**-shaped knob!"

Huey pulled the **square** knob, but this time the ship rolled over and turned upside down.

"I got it!" shouted Louie. "It's got to be the
diamond-shaped button. Hurry! Press that one!"
Huey pressed the **diamond**-shaped button. The ship
finally straightened out and got back on course.

"Hey, fellas!" shouted Louie a short while later. "Take a look at this!"

Louie pointed out the window. They were passing by the moon.

"Wow!" gasped Huey. "The moon is shaped like a **circle,** too!"

The boys' rocket raced past the moon and headed
deep into outer space. They soon came to the Planet
of the Shapes.

"Bring her in for a landing, Huey!" shouted Dewey.

Huey took the controls and brought the rocket ship
in for a beautiful soft landing.

"Wow!" exclaimed Louie. "Look at this place. Let's
go out and explore."

Huey, Dewey, and Louie left their rocket ship and began to explore the Planet of the Shapes. The first alien they met was a big red **heart**. She was with her son, a smaller blue **heart**.

"Why are you blue?" asked Huey.

"I'm afraid," said the small blue **heart**. "Afraid of the shape-eater!"

"But that's exactly why we're here!" said Huey. "You don't have to be afraid anymore! We're going to stop the shape-eater from bothering all the shape people!"

"Oh, thank you," said the big red **heart**. "We're very glad you came. Why don't you come with us and meet some of the other shape people?"

Huey, Dewey, Louie, and their new friends, the **hearts**, walked around the strange planet. They met many of the shape people. In addition to the **hearts**, they met green **circles**, orange **squares**, great big red **rectangles**, and little yellow **diamonds**.

"Wow! Look over there," said Dewey. "That shape person looks like a stop sign."

"That's an **octagon,**" explained the red **heart.**

"How about that shape over there?" asked Louie. "The one that looks like an egg."

"That's my good friend the **oval,**" said the little blue **heart.**

Suddenly all of the shape people began to run in fear. "Look out!" shouted the big red **heart**. "It's the shape-eater!"

From out of nowhere, the terrible shape-eater appeared. It began to chase the frightened shapes. The shape-eater was a big, slow-moving blob of a creature. It didn't move very fast, but it was very, very dangerous.

"Come on, fellas, we've got to save the shape people from that awful shape-eater!" shouted Huey.

Huey jumped right into the path of the shape-eater. "Hey, you big bully, leave those shape people alone!" he shouted bravely.

"I think he took your advice," said Dewey as the shape-eater turned away from the shape people.

"Yeah, but now he's headed for our rocket ship!" shouted Louie.

"Mmmm," moaned the shape-eater. "Delicious-looking rocket ship. Shape of **triangle** attached to **rectangle**!"

"Oh, no," cried Huey. "He thinks our rocket ship is lunch!"

"If he eats it, we'll never get home," cried Louie. "What are we going to do?"

"I've got an idea," said Huey. He quickly ran ahead of the creature to the rocket ship and got out a stack of colored construction paper and three pairs of scissors. "Okay, guys, start cutting!"

Huey, Dewey, and Louie began to cut the paper into all kinds of shapes.

"Because the creature moves so slowly, we should have enough time to cut out lots of shapes before he reaches our ship!" exclaimed Dewey.

"I made a blue **rectangle,**" said Huey.
"Here's a bigger **rectangle,**" said Dewey.
"My **triangle** is smaller than that," added Louie.

Soon the boys had cut out lots of shapes. The shape-eater was almost at their ship.

"Ready, guys?" asked Huey. "Start tossing!"

The boys tossed **circles, squares, triangles,** all types of shapes at the shape-eater. The hungry creature began to gobble up all the shapes.

"Look!" shouted Huey. "It's working. He's munching on those cutout shapes, and not our ship!"

A short while later Huey, Dewey, and Louie met with the shape people. "The shape-eater won't bother you anymore," announced Dewey.

"All you have to do is feed him these tasty cutout shapes," continued Louie. "He seems to like them a lot."

"We'll leave you our construction paper and scissors so you can cut the shapes out yourselves!" finished Huey.

The three boys said their good-byes, then climbed into their rocket ship and blasted off for home.

As the rocket ship landed in their backyard, the three brothers breathed a sigh of relief.

"Boy, that was some adventure!" said Huey.

"Yeah!" continued Dewey. "I'm glad we were able to help save the shape people!"

"That's right," added Louie. "I'd say that right now everything on that planet is just about shipshape!"

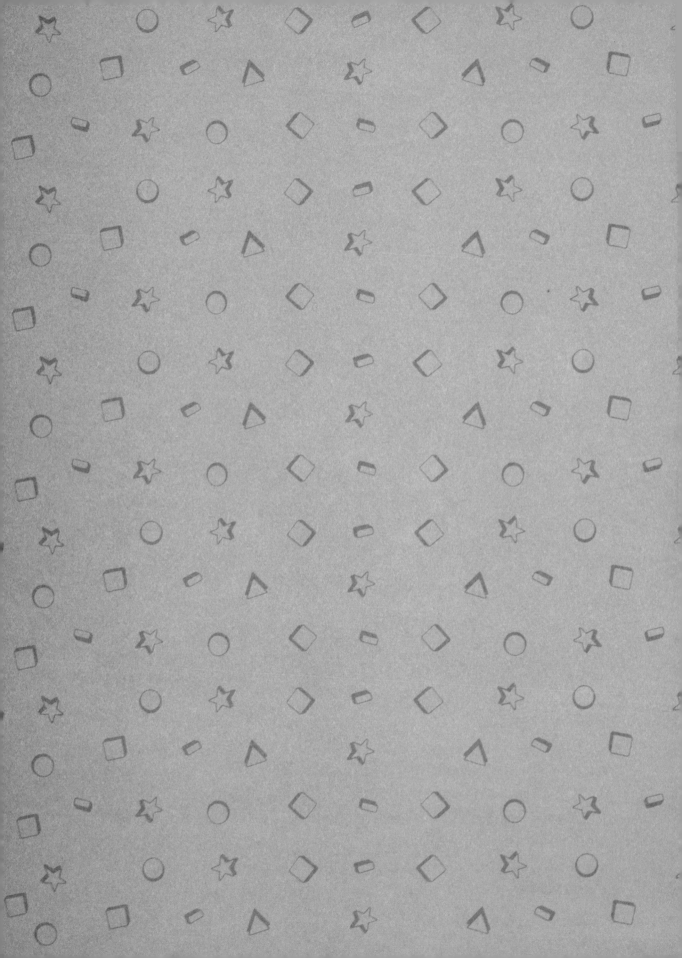